PJ Library, a program of the Harold Grinspoon Foundation
67 Hunt Street, Suite 100
Agawam, MA 01001
U.S.A.

Designed by Sabina Hahn

First Edition

10 9 8 7 6 5 4 3 2 1
052030.2K1/B1496/A8

Printed in China

ONIONS & GARLIC

Retold by Rebecca Sheir

Illustrated by Sabina Hahn

In Yiddish, "Haskel" means "wisdom."
And that was the name of a young merchant who lived in a faraway village.

Haskel's father, Anshel, was also a merchant. So were Haskel's older brother and sister, Herschel and Yentl. They all bought and sold the silkiest of silks and the wooliest of wools - the finest of all fine things.

But even though Haskel means "wisdom," his siblings called him "Haskel the Fool." It's not that Haskel wasn't smart; he was! But he was also generous and trusting – especially in the marketplace.

Everyone said they'd love to buy the whole kit and caboodle! But they'd either just spent their last dime, or they'd been robbed! So, I gave them all a discount.

Please don't call me that!

Haskel the Fool!

Haskel the Fool!

Stop!

Father, make them stop!

I'm sorry, but your brother and sister have a point.

Meanwhile, Herschel and Yentl, you are free to wander the world. I'd like to see how well you do buying and selling your goods in exotic lands.

Exotic lands?

Awesome!

Anshel ran out to the shed behind the house.
When he came back, he was dragging an enormous burlap sack.

Anshel yanked open the sack. Haskel peered inside.

The next day, Haskel boarded a merchant ship with his sack of onions in tow. But even though he tried his best to sell his onions at every port...

Before long, Haskel had to start eating
his onions just to keep from starving.

Inside the ship's kitchen, he'd scrape together whatever meal he could and throw in some onions to add more flavor. Soon, he'd found dozens of ways to use onions, like...

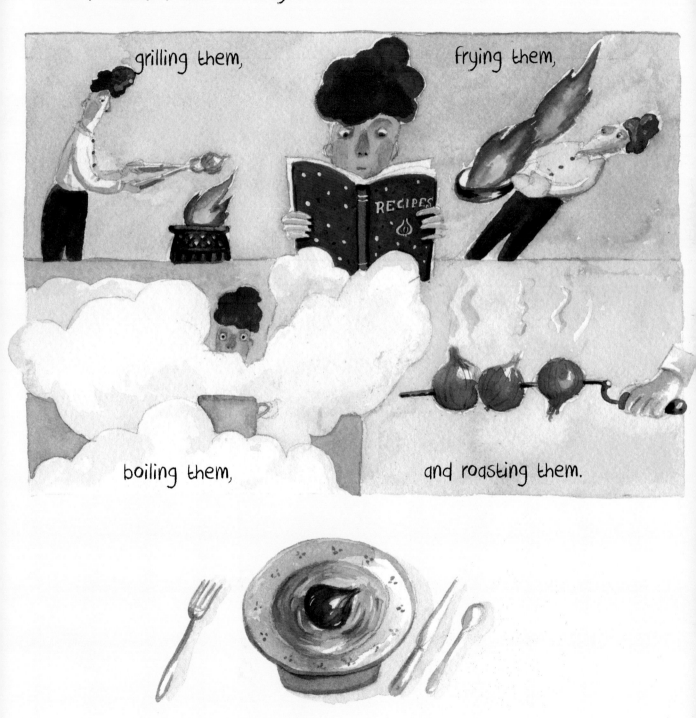

grilling them,

frying them,

boiling them,

and roasting them.

Even if his meals were meager, the onions gave them a big, bold taste.

Haskel had been at sea for many months when, suddenly, a vicious storm blew in from the north and capsized the ship!

Everyone on board was flung into the icy blue waters. Haskel clung to his sack of onions as the wind blew and night fell.

The next morning, Haskel found himself washed up on a beach. As he staggered to his feet, he felt something sharp and pointy beneath his soggy shoes.

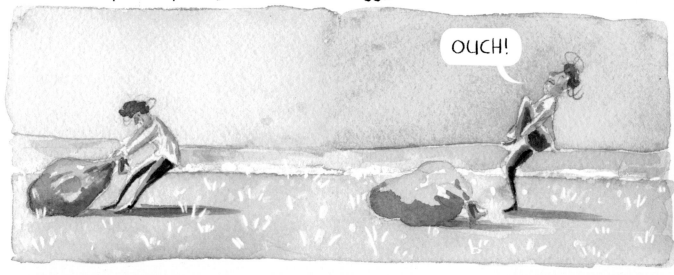

But not just one diamond: millions of diamonds! In fact,
the entire beach was covered with sparkling diamonds!
Some were tiny as a pea; others were giant as a pumpkin.
And they were all shimmering and glinting in the sun.

Well, what do you know? I'll take one of these diamonds and see if I can trade it for a meal. A nice, hot bowl of soup would hit the spot right about now.

Before long, Haskel reached a city.

He stepped inside the first restaurant he saw.

Hello, there!

I would like to order a nice, hot bowl of soup, please.

The owner of the restaurant eyed Haskel suspiciously. After all, his hair was full of seaweed and his torn clothing smelled of fish.

Oh, okay.
I guess
I'll go, then.

Listen...

You look like you've
come upon hard times.

Have a seat, and
I'll bring you a
bowl of soup.

Haskel called the restaurant owner over to the table.

Your soup is very fine - very fine, indeed.

But don't you think it would taste even better with onions?

"Onions"? What, may I ask, are "onions"?

Are you kidding? Don't you grow onions in your kingdom?

Why, no! I've never even heard of onions, let alone fed them to anybody.

Don't you feed them to your cows and rabbits and add them to your soups and salads?

Haskel couldn't believe his luck.

It just so happens I
have onions with me.

Here - taste one.

The restaurant owner popped the sliver of onion into her mouth.

Mmmmm. I've never tasted anything like this. It's so pungent! So spicy! Tell me: what can you do with these onions?

Just about anything! Like grilling them, frying them, boiling them, and roasting them. They're a very versatile vegetable, and they add such flavor.

The queen would love these onions of yours. She adores food and is always complaining that it isn't flavorful enough. You must go to the royal palace and show her this amazing vegetable.

So Haskel went to the royal palace and stood before the queen.
He told her all about onions and the many ways to cook them.

I must try these
mysterious onions
for myself.

Go, now, to the royal kitchen,
and show my chefs how to
cook with onions. Tonight,
we'll have an onion feast!

So Haskel went to the kitchen and spent hours showing the royal chefs the many ways they could prepare onions, like...

grilling them,   frying them,   boiling them,   and roasting them.

That evening, they served dish after dish to the queen.

Scrumptious!

Superb!   Mmmm-mmmm-mmm.

Tell me, young man. How many onions do you have in your sack?

Well, we used quite a few to cook tonight's meal, but I still have a good number left. And onions are very easy to grow. I can show you how to plant them. Then you can have as many as you'd like.

I will take all the onions in your sack – every last one.

What would you like in exchange?

I don't need much – just enough to get back home...

and a few diamonds?

A few? I will give you one hundred sacks of diamonds and a ship to carry you home.

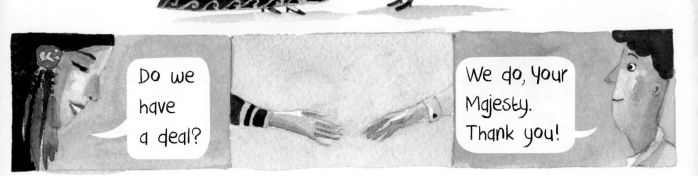

Do we have a deal?

We do, Your Majesty. Thank you!

I am so happy!

Finally, I've made a good trade!

A great trade!

Now nobody will call me "Haskel the Fool" again!

Haskel returned home with his treasures just as Herschel
and Yentl were coming back from their adventures.

When they saw his treasures, they couldn't believe
their eyes. When Haskel told them how he'd gotten
the diamonds, they couldn't believe their ears.

And when Haskel cooked them a delicious dinner that night – using, yes, onions – they couldn't believe their taste buds!

Little brother, this meal is delicious, but is it true?

Did you really find a kingdom where onions are worth more than diamonds?

It's true! I did!

Well, there's garlic.

Haskel, you're a fancy cook now. Tell us: what's another vegetable that spices up a dish?

Garlic! Of course!

We're going to bring a ship full of garlic to your kingdom, Haskel the Fool. And we'll bring back even more diamonds from your queen!

The next day, Herschel and Yentl went to the marketplace and bought all the garlic they could find. They loaded it onto the ship and set sail for the kingdom Haskel had just visited.

As they approached the palace, they passed fields and fields of a very particular crop:

Onions!

Onions!

Herschel and Yentl entered the palace and stood before the queen.

Your Majesty, we are merchants from a faraway land. We have heard you're quite fond of flavor.

"Quite fond"? I'm "quite fond" of a new dress. But flavor? I adore flavor! I'm crazy about it! The more flavor, the better!

Herschel and Yentl spent hours showing the royal chefs the many ways they could add garlic to soups, stews, and sauces.

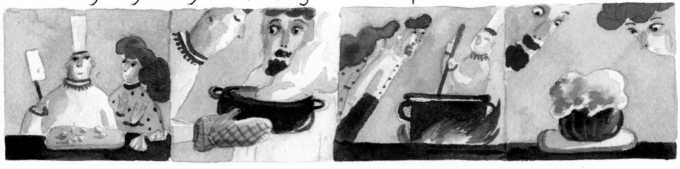

That evening, they served dish after dish to the queen.

Brilliant!

Delicious!

Nom-nom-nom-nom!

This was the question Herschel and Yentl had been waiting for.

We would like
two hundred sacks
of diamonds, Your
Highness!

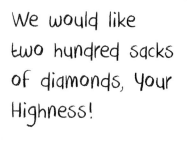

Yes, two
hundred sacks of
diamonds should
be just enough!

The next day, Herschel and Yentl boarded their ship and sailed back home. Haskel and Anshel were at the port to meet them.

Welcome back, my children!

Did you find the kingdom where they're crazy about onions?

We did!

And was the queen pleased to learn about your garlic?

She was!

In fact, she loved it!

She traded it for something even better!

But, dear brother and sister, what could possibly be better than diamonds?

Only the most precious treasure in the kingdom!

And we've waited this entire voyage to find out what it is!

Herschel, Yentl, Anshel, and Haskel all climbed down into the hold of the ship.

There, they found a giant wooden box sealed tightly with big iron nails. As Herschel and Yentl struggled to pry open the lid, they fantasized about what might be inside.

I bet it's rubies!

I bet it's emeralds!

What if it's silver?!?

Ooooh, what if it's gold?!?

Just then, the lid came flying off, and a familiar smell [...]
Because the queen had, indeed, given Herschel and Yentl [...]
precious treasure in all the kingdom. And it wasn't rubi[...]
emeralds. It wasn't silver, and it wasn't gold. No, it wa[...]
can cook and grill and fry and boil and roast. Something
that adds such flavor. Can you guess what it was?

That's right: Onions!